WELCOME TO PASSPORT TO READING

A beginning reader's ticket to a brand-new world!

Every book in this program is designed to build read-along and read-alone skills, level by level, through engaging and enriching stories. As the reader turns each page, he or she will become more confident with new vocabulary, sight words, and comprehension.

These PASSPORT TO READING levels will help you choose the perfect book for every reader.

READING TOGETHER
Read short words in simple sentence structures together to begin a reader's journey.

READING OUT LOUD
Encourage developing readers to sound out words in more complex stories with simple vocabulary.

READING INDEPENDENTLY
Newly independent readers gain confidence reading more complex sentences with higher word counts.

READY TO READ MORE
Readers prepare for chapter books with fewer illustrations and longer paragraphs.

This book features sight words from the educator-supported Dolch Sight Words List. This encourages the reader to recognize commonly used vocabulary words, increasing reading speed and fluency.

For more information, please visit www.passporttoreadingbooks.com.

Enjoy the journey!

Little, Brown and Company

Hachette Book Group
237 Park Avenue, New York, NY 10017
Visit our website at www.lb-kids.com

Little, Brown and Company is a division of Hachette Book Group, Inc.
The Little, Brown name and logo are trademarks of Hachette Book Group, Inc.

First Edition: May 2013

Library of Congress Control Number: 2012955625

ISBN 978-0-316-23440-5

10 9 8 7 6

CW

Printed in the United States of America

www.despicable.me

Passport to Reading titles are leveled by independent reviewers applying the standards developed by Irene Fountas and Gay Su Pinnell in *Matching Books to Readers: Using Leveled Books in Guided Reading*, Heinemann, 1999.

Meet the Minions

Adapted by Lucy Rosen
Based on the Motion Picture Screenplay
Written by Cinco Paul & Ken Daurio

LITTLE, BROWN AND COMPANY
New York Boston

Hi, *Despicable Me 2* fans! Can you spot these items in this book?

Minion

Dragon Kyle

Fruit

Jar

Meet Dave and Kevin and Tom
and Stuart and Jerry.
They are all Minions.

They are just a few
of the army of Minions who work
in Gru's secret underground lab!

The Minions have one job,
and one job only:
They work for Gru.

The Minions love to
carry out his master plans.
Sometimes, they do not watch out
and can make a mess.

Once upon a time,
Gru was a super villain!
He even stole the moon
with the help of the Minions!

That was before Gru became a dad
to three girls.
Now, the Minions help him
raise Margo, Agnes, and Edith!
It can be just as hard!

The Minions help
with more than the girls.
They also help Gru
with his new business.

"My life of crime is over," says Gru. "Now I am doing something sweeter. Behold, my recipe for jams and jellies!"

Dave puts up a sign that says
“Testing in Progress.”
Some Minions start to mash fruit.
Others just make a mess.

At last, a jar is complete.
Gru calls the jam
Mr. Gru's Old-Fashioned Jelly!
The Minions cheer—
until they taste it.
Yuck!

It may not be as exciting
as stealing the moon,
but Gru, the Minions, and the girls
seem pretty happy anyway.

When it is Agnes's birthday,
Gru throws her a princess party.
He invites her friends,
and they come in fun costumes.

"A dragon is coming!" says Agnes.
Kyle, their pet, is dressed up
as a dragon.

"Call the knights!" says Margo.
The Minions march out
wearing tiny suits of armor.
The Minions are the knights!

They pretend to attack Dragon Kyle.
They end up fighting one another.
Agnes laughs and tells them,
"Fight the dragon, not one another!"

The next day,
something strange happens.
A mysterious car appears
on the street.

Gru leaves the house
to check it out.
In a fiery flash, he is gone!
Someone has taken him!

Tom and Stuart
peek around the corner
just in time to see Gru disappear.
“Boss! Boss!” they shout
as the car drives away.

Tom and Stuart look at each other.
They know they have to act fast.
Gru is in trouble,
and the Minions have to help.

Tom leaps and lands on the car!
Stuart tries to jump, too,
but his suspenders get stuck.
He is pulled along.

The woman driving the car
is a secret agent named Lucy.
She spots the Minions
and captures them, too!
She zaps them with an AVL-Issued
Lipstick!

Lucy takes Gru and the Minions
to the headquarters of
the Anti-Villain League.
"Gru, we need your help," says Lucy,
"to save the world from a super villain."

Gru thinks about the job offer.
He knows his jelly tastes gross,
so he and the Minions say yes!
It will be more fun to be super spies!

Back at home,
Gru, Tom, and Stuart
tell the other Minions
about their new mission.
All the Minions cheer!

The Minions never liked
the yucky jelly anyway.
They happily smash all the jelly jars.

Gru is happier than ever.
He has a loving family,
an awesome new job,
and many Minions!